to William Forsythe & Carl Panzram

Dream Cast

Sir William Forsythe — William Forsythe or AJ Bowen

Period Sex Fred — Chris Tucker or Rik Mayall

Cop — Steven Seagal or Bruce Willis

Purr — Lisa Bonet or Janeane Garofalo

Laurie Anderson — Laurie Anderson or Lili Taylor

Michael Jackson — Michael Jackson or David Bennent

Sonic the Hedgehog — Giovanni Ribisi or Brad Dourif

Cop Son — Keanu Reeves or Michael Myers

Classic Max Headroom — Jeffrey Combs or John Glover

Henchman 2 — Al Leong

Ultimate Rot — Robert Z'Dar or Jesse Ventura

Streamline Crockett and Tubs — Don Johnson, Philip Michael Thomas or David Patrick Kelly and Tom Sizemore

David Byrne, His Squire by Force — Bruce Campbell

Ian Curtis, His Squire by Force — Ted Raimi

CIA Bill Duke — Bill Duke or Powers Boothe

Mister Gonzo Porn — Jamie Gillis or Denis Leary

Horned Vanilla Ice — Sting

Grace Jones — Grace Jones

SIR WILLIAM FORSYTHE'S FREEBASE NUPTIALS

A Screenplay

SEAN KILPATRICK

Excerpts previously published in: *Obsidian: Literature & Arts in the African Diaspora, darkfuckingwizard,* and *Black Sun Lit.*

Set in Adobe Garamond with LaTeX.

ISBN: 978-1-944697-46-4 (paperback)
ISBN: 978-1-944697-47-1 (ebook)
Library of Congress Control Number: 2017944700

Sagging Meniscus Press
saggingmeniscus.com

Table of Scenes

SIR WILLIAM FORSYTHE'S FREEBASE NUPTIALS

VHS TRACKING CORRECTS TO AN ANAMORPHIC SCROLL, IMAGES FIT INSIDE THE SUPERIMPOSING TITLE — CITY STREETS IN SPRAY PAINT MIST LIT BY HOSTILE NEON — BLAST OF TREMULOUS SUBWOOFER, BURNING BUILD-INGS, BARREL FIRES, GUNSHOTS, UNENDING CLOUD OF TEAR GAS — GANGS FLIPPING SQUAD CARS — HOOKERS SMEARING HOODS WITH THE SCALPS OF JOHNS — POLICE EXECUTING RANDOM BYSTANDERS — TEXT COM-PLETES WITH:

1992

SMASH CUT CLOSE UP—INT. WAREHOUSE

William Forsythe, sweating, fondles a gigantic cell phone.

WILLIAM FORSYTHE

Let's meet again as moguls in a life we can't remix. Nix the about-face from corporation us. If you pull the pin on this divorce, I will model a cologne that bankrupts your spirit. Whatever backs mis-ter ex-hubby's repudiated title won't eternally fucking enthrone you, crew or none, feminine wiles or mere treachery, the men you share that shan't add up that ass. Which squad you got barely crawling cuz

1

I rule out all their kidneys? Extramarital cheeseburger bitch! Somebody chap your womb? Another lactate groupie squinting through donation for his champ? *(Yanks a hair, shows it to the phone, presses phone against scar on his forehead)* This is the longest anyone'll rotate my affections. I don't believe in a world that lets us consummate. We're too perpetual. They sort our breed by muzzle flash. We purr so witch beneath the ice. Let's keep our legend slurred. I traveled with you to your first kilo and bought the machete we used to make it ours. Dedication can't vary, passed from street to leftovers. Know why I let you down, babe? I'm busy swallowing my tongue, you're that pretty. Who else coos this radioactively big? Don't I shake the napalm from your crown till even statues go extinct? *(Freebasing)* I never serve merit. My notions are puppy notions. Book me in your hysterectomy, fuckface. Listen, I neigh when I decompose. Sounds like love. *(Skeet shoots the phone. His henchmen shield away debris)* The thanks one gets. *(Second faction arrives)* Period Sex Fred! Too slick to hug! Too tall to stand!

PERIOD SEX FRED

(Handshake devolves into weird grappling) Yo, gotta address me like the company cowl? Motherfucker, don't mint your suckle if the girl split.

WILLIAM FORSYTHE

Mind your business casual ethnicity.

PERIOD SEX FRED

Missus five foot zip toppled his robust cartel. Why laud a bitch by the skeleton? I'd civilize that skank, wearily.

WILLIAM FORSYTHE

(*Aside*) Shitflake others conjecture different.

PERIOD SEX FRED

Not that she warrants postulation by the strength you ain't showing. Period Sex Fred can wait forever to taste his patients. You look tagged innermost by pain. Yet drugs are sold, sweetie.

WILLIAM FORSYTHE

My parasites are under construction. I've been loyal even to my splinters.

PERIOD SEX FRED

White gals relay efficiency upside down. Much trifle for a knick-knack. They nag you scarce.

WILLIAM FORSYTHE

Really? I can't tell someone's race unless a gun's going off.

PERIOD SEX FRED

Corny rube. Miss the concept of scaffolding at school? Come a gay amount of close. Let's inspect what's formerly your face. *(They tap foreheads)* Yo. You can't mingle without a fucking receipt. Why the need to domineer a bitch? Submit yourself vulnerable for something matched and ingest the subsequent nightmare time again. That's my relationship status. Their cruelty is admirable because they never mean it. We're purely intentional. They flawlessly just are. Don't hold onto her like a dork. People forsake. Men, we're professional fuck ups, but we're professional at it. I know she punk'd you with success she had on loan. Check the great aid for advancement, this general lack of ethics the puritans collared women with. Be above a witch hunt. They steal your fuel that way, brother. I want to see you killing folks correct. Those mostly blue. Remember walkie-talkie assholes? We shrink the badge daily. Nor are we aware of morality, unless suffering under someone's misuse of it. *(Cracker voice)* Then may a privileged response rationalize a puny indignity. Women struggle to placate because it's not engendered in them to accept their handicapable needs. Let them off the hook for being beautiful. Say goodbye once in awhile. Once a month for me! Don't force her to spend the ten seconds necessary to replace you. No one alive is equal. There are no rights. We keep fucking nodding, don't we?

WILLIAM FORSYTHE

Sir, you're shipshape enough I want to sum you up with a bowtie. Advice so profitable my lover's tears won't stay herpetic in their holster. *(Long pause, they smile, shotgun explodes from William Forsythe's trench coat, scalping Period Sex Fred. The factions open fire)* Sorry I unzipped you at your most fucking Buddha! Pizzazz is leaking by the nickel! Always wanted a convertible! *(Holding the scalp in place)* Salute what she did. Allow me to continue your sponsorship, sown to the result. I ushered you through college on a whim. True mafia went institution. Brilliant chemist, formulator of bonds like a ripcord for the community. *(Freebasing into Period Sex Fred's head wound, sticking the scalp down with duct tape during seizure)* Fucking girlfriends! They consistently pencil in the chivalrous.

Police surround the building. Machine gun volley, faction on sports bikes crashing into product, exploding cocaine fog, police ripped apart, exotic birds disturbed from the rafters, synthesizer score pounding. A cop performs complicated karate.

WILLIAM FORSYTHE

(Observing Cop) This piece of shit keeps orgasming in his tourniquet. He leaves his garden hose on on the sidewalk. This mother-

fucker dribbles snow. He bothers alarm clocks, but I'm the bastard woke up screaming. Nijinsky hopped out of bed constitutionally bound. He believes his ballet. The self-same squabble: any pimp's subscription to their own cause. Got some petrified son staying home? He's totally your money explaining itself, faggot. Nothing sates a proper dweeb. I promise those kempt free of crime never sate. Never deal with their veneer. Couldn't breech the object as it destroys you for the best. No hero's ever swapped their merchandise for heart. Declare that shit a thump without cliché. Think he elates his pets wealthier than their bowl? Spiffy about life? A bit of thwarted glory nine to five? You are trained and borrowed merely from the world. *(Cop has cleared the room)* Am I on? *(Rushes Cop and is flipped, freebasing on floor)* Which fucking juice box did you administer?

COP

You one of the tawny chicklets I collect today? Offer me plump discourse concerning your almighty self? Guess a trickle gets shit done. Your calamity charts indignant like a lone teen more hot pink instinct than contribution. I'm the pimp your woman needs a household about. I leash a pup of your ilk, his demeanor fixed equally pouty. Additional wife and mistress feeding themselves space. Rather clasp reef on the union's dime. Buddy, no fear. They'll be knocked vertical again in honor of the world. There's a lot of who

6

and how swimming below my belt. The public won't extend your credit from a sandwich bag. Seems the fluids you pop out weather their Ziplock. Pounce through these cuffs before they get sexy. Why you buckwheat tinkerbells always too spacious to sneak back up mom? Eh? How many renegades to a sphincter in here? *(Absently moving his arm where Period Sex Fred stands moaning)* Try guessing my pulse.

WILLIAM FORSYTHE

(Flicking resin in Cop's eyes, blocking his counter, collapsing onto him, punching him unrecognizable) Welcome to the rest of your keloid! *(Burst)* Let's swap medical histories. Flavor these dentures plain as compromise, bitch. *(Burst)* I will jot your family into their pizza. Molest the fucking blacksmith that forged your badge. I can tell your bladder's glazed. *(Burst, retrieves tooth fragment from Cop's throat)* Oh, the filling's intact. Make a wish. Wish you didn't smudge my friend. You condemn his hygiene with your gossipy paw. Was taking his temperature your first experience? There's a pardon ready, if you scurry to comb his orientation. Who dusts off your bacon? Who gets in there and sweeps? I bet even your psychologist calls you bulletproof. How many loved ones you dismiss a day? *(Short burst, exhausted)* Anyway, I'll microwave your fucking shield! Phew. *(Chucks Cop's walkie-talkie at the wall)* The fancier the tattletale, the more it's everyone. Sorry, I give up on fidelity with a girl and I'll lose

my body count. *(Helps him stand, dusts him off, kicks him walking)* Stroll, pinecone.

EXT. STREET

William Forsythe, double Uzis, indiscriminate fire, cop cars crashing, shoving dazed Cop up front, dragging him on sidewalk, holding hands, towing Period Sex Fred behind.

WILLIAM FORSYTHE

(Picks clumped, rat-chewed hamburger from gutter) Hey, who put Pac-Man to sleep? On level crisp. Huh? Irradiate your petticoat area. *(Rubs burger on Cop)* Hail the apparatus, you fucking colleague! Our gruel has excessive fine print! Freelance plebe grease. I speak of the silverfish going up you. They don't love mean, they love often. I'll pitch you the spectrum. Sire a goddamn lottery down below. *(Bites burger)* What a spouse. Woe is my errant gender. Yum, gender was once relevant. No family affords its ideal. *(Savoring)* My chemicals are ruined and better. It tends to your germs. Soothes before it says. *(Presenting burger in chopper light)* Some crusaders expect necrophilia from the horizon. *(Burger is shot from his hand)* Whirlybird's menacing our harvest! *(Rips a hose from the dirt and lassos the helicopter's landing skid)* I reverse gentrified the out-lip mole you're touring, reared neon to enamel. Smell this prime fucking turf? We

bootleg central heating. I refer to the civic part of your shoe. When a service is rendered or a paycheck's earned, my hard-on loses attendance. Let's frolic through the starvation peekaboo! *(Shoves crackpipe in hose, flame spiraling vertically until the sniper ignites, dropping to the street)* Ever try opening an umbrella in the fact that you exist? We're kind of sitting ducks in stereo, like homo sapiens mistakenly evolved a consciousness, the squish-pattern echo of big bang, onward from stasis, our synapses just disguised, itinerant star guano death rattling. We have a great talent for carrying ourselves from magic to fertilizer. I'm all about our full potential as fertilizer, but that's too optimistic. *(Pools finger in sniper's ash)* I represent the holes in my costume. Swarm them, mashed potatoes on repeat. You never been bereaved. *(Crosses Uzi muzzles to sear and swab an Ash Wednesday sign on Cop's forehead)* I can't help but to throttle whatever lets me worship it. Loss is the religion perched cordial as a phoenix behind each citizen. Hamstring the whole enchilada before a cuddle takes on debt. I boost my princess higher than the goals she set for me. Now I can soil myself for the length of a president. No item will betroth her. Picture any empire built on quicksand. You're likewise disemboweled by TV. Tiling the roof or vice versa. Wife bored into the nap we call trust. I vow to rape her in front of all your purchases.

INT. PURR WAREHOUSE

Purr snorts coke through a diamond straw, pinkie fingernails are long and sharp. Henchmen unload crates. William Forsythe throws Cop at Purr's feet, ties the leash he's made to a henchman.

WILLIAM FORSYTHE

Boy, sure hope nobody skimmed Marx. Pinko's pubes tore the fucking maxi pad. *(Henchmen laugh)* We'll stack the skittish for allegiance. Whichever rinky-dink musketeer handles choice. Omit lady stunt bra with a crane shot. I'm querying you gents. Follow papa. Even if my blowjob ain't as flush. Her mood swings won't hold a target fatter than your craft.

Purr motions to her henchmen. They do not respond.

WILLIAM FORSYTHE

A diminishing meow. You're worse off than the cross around your neck. Someone snuck away with her Skittles. She's ticked. Is your arena wispy of a sudden? We mustn't glower without lube. The rectally whiskered may protest. I think kids tumble from there, right? Of course, if one currently did, we'd page a mortician to milk you. Bounce straight pulverized at mankind. I only kiss a son of a bitch to place them underground. *(Snorts her coke)* At least your product's sweet. Shit's the pinnacle. It supposed to reissue belly buttons this hard? *(Period Sex Fred shuffles between them and shits on the floor. Purr tenses her posture)* Congratulations! Didn't realize you two were expecting. Maybe the crib's bulkier than all outside. Ever make the crowd strip with you? Ever forfeit someone your throne and they construct theirs right next door? Ever feel vulnerable under tanning lights? Standing still ever entirely fucking discolor you? *(Purr hugs Period Sex Fred)* I flake the manicure you'd rather fuck? I would have lapped the straw rot from your mohawk! *(Aims at her)* Stop hugging him! He's mine now! He's capable of returning above a meek percentage of the love he's given! He's not the chump it would take to deserve you! Don't scrounge in the manure you've reduced us to, cunt.

Purr approaches William Forsythe and balances on his shoulder, removing her boots. Henchmen aim at her. Purr slices off a portion of the skin around her ankle with her pinkie and hands it over, smiling, whispery.

PURR

Can't tiptoe backward through your diarrhea without leaving prints.

Tattoo of a satanic symbol visible under the blood, William Forsythe presses over the same tattoo on his wrist. Exiting, Purr kisses a henchman.

WILLIAM FORSYTHE

(Choked up, calling after) I never meet anyone with a name, so I name them. You're called Purr because being born is no excuse and the preceding boredom is no excuse!

Kissed henchman presents his neck to William Forsythe, who stabs a hole wide enough for his fist and reaches in, absently carrying henchman around, searching knuckle deep inside his throat.

WILLIAM FORSYTHE

I'm pawing over shit you said to corner her lipstick. Gotta audition for your flatline, boy. That a cough or your g-spot inflate? Hmm, ultra squirrelly basehead dispatch at play. Nice that as a child you brewed sun tea with grandma. *(Henchman wetting pants)* He's performed a misdemeanor in the sauna. Come on, shovel forth her poise. Ah, she's present for once, shied and tamed. Watch those comely zzz's do cursive. Hi, darling. You're my confederate souvenir trached by the kiln. Please spell longevity before you hobnob. Ask your cum to beeline. None hanker less clad than us. Bring out the cave shit, baby.

COP

(Tied to a chair) Coward.

WILLIAM FORSYTHE

What, him? Everyone dies far too endured. *(Henchman hits floor)* Tut-tut. *(Grabs Cop's ears)* Daddy owns the head you owe him.

COP

Your tantrum got extra innings? That girl that dumped you, downtown we prize her for chow.

WILLIAM FORSYTHE

(Unwraps a sheath of pink fiberglass insulation) Heh. Dude's saying he autographed her PMS with a sippy cup.

COP

(Slapped with insulation) Ow. You slapping me with fiberglass insulation?

WILLIAM FORSYTHE

(Strafes insulation over Cop's face, unrolls duct tape) I learned this trick from my obstetrician. *(Using tape to rip shards of glass from Cop's face, shows sparkling strip to henchmen)* A tad of treasure for the swoon.

HENCHMAN

(William Forsythe begins bleeding into his moustache, all henchmen's noses bleed) Boss?

WILLIAM FORSYTHE

I found Purr in an alley, snuggling glass, thong of scar tissue, hating men as she should. Organs inched around inside her during hugs. Where you at inside? Appendectomies everywhere. Little tag team villain rode my shoulders. A week hence, her assailants were bowing to their cartilage. We crocheted a yipping carpet under our damp patch. This was art, not revenge: no difference. We got beauticious with each other. Her hate was retroactive. She could stare you into cancer. Why's power inevitably excuse relationships? We had to honeymoon in our carrion, addicts of the same casket. Girl, what's the fucking planet's exit strategy if I can't win you back?

EXT. STREET

Purr glides rigid along the sidewalk, outstretched fingers, makeup smeared into war paint. Men by a barrel fire follow her.

MAN

Peep this forest fire pussy! Bald with angst. A limited order thereof no paper towel refutes! But okay. Your smirk die off? Why so glum, ma'am? If I ran the plantation, you'd be its mime. I lug an anchor of dick blood per diem, cutie pie. It'll up your brownie points. I'll foist you in a bassinet. Then we're all playing doctor with each other's kids. I'd prowl the top unreachable section of your chamber pot. Damn, please retire upwind. You asleep between the ears? Bet you could spit shine a T-Rex. What's your name, antiques shopper? Is squatting your quandary? 'Cause I fuck like the globe's solution. You of a mind, bitch? *(Switchblade)* I'm done tripping over hello.

PURR

(Pops her pinkie through his labrum) Bye. I decorate my glove with your lukewarm passing. Wave yourself goodbye. *(Man waves at his own face)* You're finished standing up to pee, the significant breadth. I can't sneeze of late without castrating somebody. You should oxidize your testicles before they skip away. I'll turn them clapping simulcast for cake. I'm that careful of a spinster fluke. Sing into your friend's trophy. *(Man jabs the switchblade into his friend's shoulder. The friend kneels so Purr can pop her other pinkie into his labrum and leads them, crouched, her new arms, chained tandem)* I hurt my boys' feelings to see if they'll try. Is your business card you quivering? We can't network till you've bled out. I don't mean to antagonize you. I wouldn't antagonize a sleeve. I only introduce myself inside a fellow. *(Helicopter spotlight)* The sun got mislaid, contracted the blueprints for a spark. It was pregnant with me, back when pregnancy was a

thing. You had to close your eyes to reach gravity. There is no lucent doing I concur with. No such glow. Unless my scars twinkle when I screw. I was homeschooled with a brick, potty trained on the curb. Who don't roll the sidewalk in their tampon?

POLICE LOUDSPEAKER

Apologies for the inconvenience! Anybody's a catwalk aficionado from this height. You're however I like my lettuce. I could draw you a map doggy style. I'd reposition my children's college fund on that lap. I find indifference sequential to the use of air. Perhaps I could dunk myself in you like a tactful guest? May we disregard a chromosome or two?

PURR

(Stares upward, her arms pointing in a chain as she does) Come closer. *(Sniper jumps out of the helicopter. Purr steps in his mess)* My slippers punctuate my feet. The clingiest gullet direct to boring. You gotta brush me until my plague's glossy or I won't like you. Prolong or nothing materializes. *(The men, as her arms, set the sniper's hair on fire with cracklighters)* Mankind's amplest heresy was attaching wheels to the flame. Ya'll been escaping reverence ever since. I have no ancestors because they said leave fire where the lightning landed. *(Directs her men into a lean. Blood from their mouths and noses extinguishes the skull and Purr pats and collects his ashes with her feet)*

Too much puffy, not enough downfall. No amount of smoke will let you ostrich out the stars. Can't gauge magic under such a locomotive backlog of policies, boy. You want to clump each other up. Can't make the source of your warmth another fucking inventory. You're just mad because technology neutered you. I forgive that you might only rediscover your body in mine. But you may not cure the maps I make.

INT. LAURIE ANDERSON, THE ONE AND ONLY'S WAREHOUSE

Geocentric spirals of women, robed and bowing, intoning spells, legs parted so their periods flow along grooves in the floor, collected in a centralized fountain. Laurie Anderson, the One and Only, wearing a white suit, having changed her hair more Annie Lennox-like in a previous artistic compromise to support and attract Purr, background elevator music that annoys her, corrects her Menstrual Cult's postures with a violin bow. Each member resembles Purr. Purr detaches her arms, throws them at Laurie Anderson, the One and Only's feet. The men become aware of their surroundings, afraid.

LAURIE ANDERSON, THE ONE AND ONLY

(*Voice modulator*) Oh, entrez vous. Your presence has quite the undue influence on our humidifier. I earmarked all your hairballs. Beloved whose luteum boggles compatibility, do you still ovulate like a grand piano? Sport a bundle doubly afloat in the viable mustache of your license plate? Are we brining new arrivals with a placemat right on the bust of whomsoever? I never implied anything's plural or hammered home an annunciation that wasn't meant for me alone. Have your residencies been peaking elsewhere? Is anyone capable of recognizing a vigil created in their honor? Remember how fortunately we beeped? We're so tame without you. I'm always mistaken for a boss. Till you swing by and forsake me. Your merest phone booth infantry. I'm going to love you with less purse this time. My dinged up coloring book, subtract the guarantee. My ate crayon. Who would dare refund you? *(They smile)* Don't let's speak to the revenge of a recommended smile. Before the inquisition, I should blush. You mewl for none. Takes a lot of crime to keep you.

PURR

(Embracing Laurie Anderson, the One and Only, motions to the men)
I refuse to put in an appearance, unless a sacrifice is at hand.

LAURIE ANDERSON, THE ONE AND ONLY

(To men) We need the sum total of your sperm by accident. *(Men sneer to each other. Laurie Anderson, the One and Only embeds a dagger in the floor between them, without looking)* Use the donation kit.

Men, crying, line the skin of their balls against the floor and saw, gentle.

PURR

I'm asking for the type of support that really matters. One that comes with artillery.

LAURIE ANDERSON, THE ONE AND ONLY

He tries to marker property lines on you. He's just a big boy you should shirk. Together we can tie a ribbon around anyone's plot. We invalidate compasses here.

PURR

I want him to receive my armies by the hangnail.

LAURIE ANDERSON, THE ONE AND ONLY

We need an anthropomorphic provider prefaced by the word duh. Grimace hit a homerun with his stuffing. Load program gynecological mascot. Technology culminated in Pap smears. They scrambled us tolerant. Soon computers will fit us. Can we elude the moon, traipsing left and right? Clearly the moon planted her flag on us. *(Dips Purr in a kiss)* I long to purr right through your miscarriages. Beg their permission when I want. Till I'm the steep plaintiff thirsting to heave you. I miss you with more rabid calories than my metabolism may confess. Double knot your blindfold because this costuming can really gobble. *(Steps on dagger, finishing the castrations, men screaming, passing out, and tosses their squashed, seminal-dripping mess in the center of the period fountain, causing a large computer monitor to rise)* We go poof all day. Hand-me-down hors d'oeuvres formatted for compact disc. Let the cursor be our birthright. *(Taps her hands together, lights shine red through her flesh)* We're more DNA than idea.

CLASSIC MAX HEADROOM

(Looping onscreen) Are we live? Well, if I age by the percent. What I wanna know is, how many lightbulbs does it take to screw in a lesbian? This crowd might stake my ratings on a buzz cut. What's wrong, honey? You leave your blinker on and call it stardom? Were I the hero of this novel, I'd be feces. There's no gesture too prehistoric when you beg for an excuse. Reeks here as if the fauna were caught in their broom.

LAURIE ANDERSON, THE ONE AND ONLY

Yep, we've been bargaining at the hospice again. He's the Lamborghini of chronic diphtheria. Massive cum swig data, daddy old school, pillar of central sciences when they're juiced. The capital therein could erode Pepsi. Humor him as you would any master. He surfs with a choir for backup.

CLASSIC MAX HEADROOM

(*Horrendous laugh*) Pay no attention to the WASP behind the curtain, missy. Be nice or our avatars might repent. Don't you hear culture? It beats off to your threshold. They set the prince of crack on fire inside TVs for less a dance. Someone taught their parrot way too much Shakespeare. The sighs I dispense commission their own broker. Perhaps your vitals come with choice of dressing?

LAURIE ANDERSON, THE ONE AND ONLY

Women duped men into running the buildings they built us. Yet, who's trapped in perfume? These bodies are auctioned from their copyright. My creditors included the option to sparkle.

CLASSIC MAX HEADROOM

Not everyone treats their tampon like a squib. Don't ban pads in order to continue. I'm the last grant from team juggernaut willing to bend your makeup over.

LAURIE ANDERSON, THE ONE AND ONLY

(*Gestures to fountain*) Isn't our Faberge deft? Only drains withstand mankind. Our sewage is so present tense. I count little Reagans in my sleep. Watch him grin, patent pending.

CLASSIC MAX HEADROOM

If I showed you what I have down there, your bleach would fall out. Get farting under my vowels. Sorry, I can't stop being short with myself. You mustn't nag a circuit, dear. I'm very regardless. The bloodstain that requires batteries. Be a numb cog or I'll trash your gym membership.

LAURIE ANDERSON, THE ONE AND ONLY

I stalked my babysitter until she cancelled her foundation. Her and her innumerable boyfriends hardly bequeathed the yeast to form an exit sign. How much do I deploy before you assist the spank? Are we an adjustable potentate?

CLASSIC MAX HEADROOM

Chill, your tank's on layaway. It has features. Nobody crammed a finish line in your glucose, so don't go tearing up on cable access. Your foot soldiers will arrive giftwrapped with a CIA sprinkler set. I'll be the cause of any war because I'm a journalist at heart. Brother, can you spare a ticker? It should pump Cool Ranch.

PURR

(Removes blindfold) I get it. Anyone with a credit card is a fucking celebrity. Your urethral array's too conjugal to visit. Take up flirting with whoever spays you? You stoop to his gluttonies. Which impotent future failed our applause? Is this the hell where Satan put us on furlough back inside our bodies? Should I tattoo a kitchen over my wet spot? Must we be tarred and feathered by the bean? No reprieve from the gnomes chasing my G-string. I'm lonely for nuclear winter under the lordly ex's figmental thumb. You had to breathe his meat. But the swaddling asphyxiating you was palpably spent.

CLASSIC MAX HEADROOM

Geeze.

LAURIE ANDERSON, THE ONE AND ONLY

You suggest I sterilize my acumen for the genuine article? Unstick those pixels. *(Classic Max Headroom disappears)* I sculpt a milestone a minute, you prick. Your anger goes folkloric. How about: should we mud wrestle until my uterus is bloodshot? You're so quintessential no exam will pass you. Keep my swill in mind. Be its head honcho. Don't be a trinket for the already customized. See why we tapered off, Purr? I've blown out my pelvic floor cheering for you. I'm barely worth this henhouse because how penultimate we seemed. Truncated waistline is what they let me advertise. Quick to scold in favor of appetite. Yes, they put our eggs in a vending machine. Always someone's costlier pain embarrasses yours. The big American problem is we never bow.

PURR

(Bows) Forgive me. I've been harassed by the self-appointed knights of pop. My kill list is heavier than me and I plan to eat more of it than I weigh.

LAURIE ANDERSON, THE ONE AND ONLY

Please remain of no use to a world that calls passion weak because it wants parts. Utilitarian gratitude disgraced our entire biology. Wow. Haven't had my feelings hurt since I met you. We were trying on diapers at the same yard sale. Forever ago I stopped dueling the efficiency with which everything I love gets stolen. You need multiple partners because it would take a bazooka to interrupt you. *(They laugh)* I'll loan you my clones, girl. They got frosting on top. I fashioned them from men so they could die notching each other off. The sockets where their hearts were don't whistle at the bottle return.

Spotlights from ceiling, three opponent bosses. Ultimate Rot, steroid needles hanging off him, in wrestler speedo, face paint, mullet and armband streamers. CIA Bill Duke, suit and silenced pistol, perpetual growl, and Mister Gonzo Porn, rings and necklaces, Hawaiian shirt, shouldering a video camera.

LAURIE ANDERSON, THE ONE AND ONLY

(Rubbing oil on Ultimate Rot's chest) Superstition was gloating in us

before the ocean left on holiday. That's why my conclusions are all backwash. I've developed a penchant for the bogus. This one spawns on a slant abacus. The beanstalk in his trousers murders clouds. That one could sketch the cosmos with a braid. He can shoehorn how flat the universe is into your allowance. And the closer spiels coed revenues from VHS. Whose plight brushes skirts this up? I'm steady as soon as I'm beholden. You boys ready to lead the honest on their tour straight back inside the vacuum? Listen, Socrates is heehawing through his death penalty. He's been condemned to do solos. Render him an intermission sans latrine. Everybody's exterior's chummy, but there's no joke sharp enough to poke a hole in our incubator. You can't spank the gourmet with a lightbulb. Can't raise a billboard for your nap. Derive us an appropriate touché. Pleather's another sonnet to my touch. Even the pearly gates are cubic zirconia. Believe the impersonation first!

INT. FORMER PURR WAREHOUSE

William Forsythe huddles around Purr's boots, tapping freebase ash into them. Nosebleed and pipe residue smear him like Goth makeup. Bugs he occasionally swats have begun to circle him and increase throughout.

WILLIAM FORSYTHE

I puke my own sawdust. Sweetbreads turn me in the aisle. I just gorge on crusts and never dream. Lose sleep to your purpose. Love's always the other person's symptom. I moored her by the scruff. We could not doze in each other's presence. Weird how genuinely unaffected by pussy you have to be to retain it. Every evil hides a want for comfort. Be a meat with me, she said. There is no kind of food that wants without aging. *(Period Sex Fred sneezes maggots and begins breakdancing. Blood from his head creates a circle as he windmills. Henchmen get sprayed and do not react)* Look at me, I gotta make myself some girl's girl or I can't ticker tape. Towels risk mold to clean you. No one dots their colonizer's shamrock and means it. How sad for the roving bought. How itchy. I cramp up about the indigenous. Let's let our hands be baked inside their puppets. We'll snack ourselves assimilated. I'm the aftermath of white. I don't stamp what I ransack. I swab fraud on my surroundings and those perishable as a consequence are commoditized with no other motive but to have the hug returned. And, oh boy, if you don't. *(Admires Period Sex Fred)* B-boy whups his vessel. I'm not packing the buckshot to possess that. You pommel horse motherfucker. You're my traction. *(Stops him spinning)* I like to waddle, even when I'm sneaky. Best man doing a handstand. Jilt me with your illest ills. We got the head of the beast in our clutches tonight. Tell my smithereens hi. *(Points at Cop)* He loiters clumsier than Europe. Delusions of grandeur when he migrates. Who's to redeem the vacancy in my whore? You two should hump your contour into plastic. Apparently, the castaway I'm kooky for coached you both how. I pick you, captain oink, as my bronze medal bride. I flogged my pig out of wedlock. We'll operate under such bigamies. Is it true we stood in traffic to meet? Am I trolling you into a demolished curtsy? Care to become utterly gulped? Shall we rewind our gauze together? Ain't we sizable and ad-libbed. You could hang a hanger off our clits right now. Scarf the twat through a megaphone. *(Grabs Cop and kisses him, both their mouths bleed)* I fucked all my action figures to death because they wouldn't love me. *(Breaks a glass casing on the wall and removes a gun with bride and groom figurines attached to the muzzle)* Break in case of bitch. The one till death I can rely on. Magician's saw caught rabies. Seek therapy while my tarantulas giggle. The purpose of a gun is civilization shouldn't have to be so inherently mandatory. A gun in your mouth solves that. Civilization, you know, the failed concept that human decency can be stretched beyond the interval of a half-made effort? I'm so ambitiously nonfunctional mosquitoes reject my scraps. You wanna press charges on me you're going to have to solve for nope. City don't have the taxes to pursue. Especially if I smooch toilet wine in your siren. I bet your genetic code was traced. We'll find out after I ram the acoustics off your firstborn. I take my crushes literally. *(Snapping fingers at henchmen)* Which hench produced the script for silverware? Did the hospital issue your mom a summons? Trying to have a meltdown here. Shit's becoming indelible. *(On bended knee before Cop)* Cheers to our longstanding troubles. Sorry there's no engagement stone. I couldn't fit a barn around your finger.

Henchmen retrieve and shove a bridal dress over Cop's head. William Forsythe shoots the marriage weapon into the rafters, sprinklers go off, Michael Jackson, the Prince of Crack, face taped on, small and waxen, burnt and smoking, fitted waist deep inside a hollowed television box, begins to descend.

COP

(Muffled) Fair to say this ensemble will billow in your digestive tract before the end credits?

WILLIAM FORSYTHE

Your evidence is all dial tone. Besides *(manipulates Cop's bearings through the dress)*, we're where the credits go to end.

MICHAEL JACKSON, THE PRINCE OF CRACK

Cool it! Aww, Willy, you're a study in backlash minus the prerequisite of success. Well, you're basically minus everything. Do you feel incapable of tenderness? Wait, don't answer. I want you to pretend you grew up somewhere. Life is tragedy plus rhinestones. Dad seared my eyes, using spooky peroxides, until they were a haunting of his own. He expunged their velour because I was given birth to without an agent. They thawed me from a block of regurgitated twins. I was the most beautiful marionette in the pile. Being handed a name was my first molestation. I was later told the actual crime was my mother's cunt ever splitting its membrane. But it's cool that I live in this country, because I found a way to amputate my black. More leg room if you falsify your eunuchdom. From diapers to shrillest fame, boy, dad shrieked. Even my pets had visiting hours. I loaded flute registers into what humanity calls a throat and the fucking tabloids sang instead. They cuckolded me with the first rodent I fell for. We met under the kitchen table, snickering with confidential cheese. We had a choice strychnine sprinkled on our cobbler. I hid him in the hydrogen they tampered through my suits. But the hoi polloi is skilled at butchering a recluse. They felt taunted by my income and circled him, damn transphobic pieces of confetti. He was seized round his consoling tail, such a bitty nummers, the shah of mice, and trampled into the next ointment for cellulite. For lunch, I wept a saucer full. The hunted usually find it a bummer. They stole my baby like there was no such thing as rape. I carved his maze into my face. I wasn't stingy with his phantom. Choruses featuring his onomatopoeic dynasty were brought to pass. I became the commerce of my frown. I could recite my creature by the follicle. Top twenty rotten peach, fluffed for lack of a pillow, rumpled in fantasies of him returning. Million dollars per nervous breakdown. And if they didn't consume, all people did was insist on crops anyway. Wherever I fled, there were balloons behind me. *(Yelling at invisible paparazzi)* Go ahead and install a balloon animal between my legs, if you can afford the wedding! I was high off in memoriam, fusing him to the safest pop. Impossible to grab your own crotch, if you're schizophrenic. Talk about inner struggle. I head south and, bam, I'm a gentleman. Some kids got in the way, due to size. They had to understand how even the animals on their pajamas would someday die. Brats rifled through my boo's peewee loafers, capturing nada. There were offspring brimming in my mittens, the studs of which journeyed a speck of the Sabbath. Naw. My hate is the diamond that jewels back. I'm a robot painted into fame with the dust of its own tears. A sparkling scream in favor of child labor laws. I haul a lactose smooth as magazines. I had no choice but to be brilliant. To gesticulate until I was a fucking rat too. Mutilate me ripe again, treated decent this time. I gotta mug like someone ditched their mortgage on humus. Why leave me this much a virgin? Yeah, I wrung out cradles. Peddled bogue monopolies behind the zipper. I come like a William Blake reprint, if the newspaper mandates. My orientation is dirt. I wanna grind on ground. Spoon earth till I'm more under it than I already am, I fuck like hell gives out trophies. You can only judge me if we're playing Russian roulette. The deeper I apologize for them, the sexier my crimes. Wanna make our stenographers die of shame?

WILLIAM FORSYTHE

(Bows) My liege, I said I do too soon. Canst we mail order a better half with a more exploitable lope? This one's so naïve he might backpedal his consent.

MICHAEL JACKSON, THE PRINCE OF CRACK

Consent? Tee hee. *(Pets Cop)* Recipients that revolve consent void consent. Can't get sworn in as a priest because my scales ain't showing. *(Scribbles on own face with black marker, sniffs it)* I dyed myself your great black trope. Not that puns aren't the sole language we're ambushed by. Words flail me. I was cursed to never be booed. Technically impossible to jeer my moves. You're only as immortal as your cinematographer's competence. No, I dig not having to hiccup entrepreneurially. Let's tuck in our shed. *(Sloughs flesh off his arm, shapes it into powdered squares, and lights it off his smoking head)* I'm the pure shit. Cut me with twenty-four karat baking soda or my configuration will cause a famine in your worms. Freebase was a religion the second flint rock met itself. I'm set up to knight you. *(Knights William Forsythe's shoulders with crackpipe, they hit it)* I dub thee Templar who does Kung Fu into his handkerchief. If I was permitted an afro pick, I'd stab you with it. Luckily, my hairdo's a mural. Rise, if cremation evened out your accolades.

SIR WILLIAM FORSYTHE

Scope out bridezilla, his constipation's waning gibbous. I don't have enough hemorrhoids to paint your portrait, but the one I wield could fill a parking garage. *(Blowing smoke in Cop's face)* Seems like a mere forty-five minutes ago we were exchanging coy glances across the slaughterhouse. What monumental teenagers we are. I like you. I like how none of what you say or do or think much matters. It endears me to you. Don't interrupt the shudder by responding. We gotta flop around love won't speak its name. Love like a kind of stroke we had together.

MICHAEL JACKSON, THE PRINCE OF CRACK

Tick tock, fatty. The party hats are peeling atop their perms. We have much squealing to do. Shucks, whose kids am I kidding? What clock wouldn't donate both hands to spank it to you? Ugh, which brand of advice strangles us the quietest? *(Whips out bible with a dance jerk)* Dearly departed, clout of Séraphitüs, approximate our queernesses. Flip us off as soon as we maintain. Gather through our circulation the mummy grain we smoke to heal sniffles. You guys are my favorite incumbent wank. A Polaroid of toiletries couldn't toast my house as good. *(Period Sex Fred pelts Cop with shit dingleberries from his pants)* Halt the wedding rice! *(Flings bible with a dance jerk)* We mustn't take a bicycle pump to his sinuses without rooting up the shattered family some petty insurance will too readily compensate.

SIR WILLIAM FORSYTHE

Don't spit on my cake and call it frosting, because I'll eat that too, starting with your mouth.

MICHAEL JACKSON, THE PRINCE OF CRACK

You thought you would attend prom inside his child without my canned laughter behind you? Are you a stout enough hustler to seriously offend me? His bloodline shouldn't have a third act. Is my Jheri curl sweat too lavish for his son? Back him into mine. Don't pinch nobody unless it leads to the death of schools! I don't make babies, I cause a flood. *(Winks)* Bring me the infant I used to be, eyes wavering on their stalks. When I lisp, you fetch the impediment. My velveteen testicles give me thumbs down on any greater sentience. Still, let's dismiss one into nudity. I feel its teeth coming in yellow. Speaking of blue balls…

Michael Jackson, the Prince of Crack opens a tabernacle. Sonic the Coke Mule spins out, grinding and unsticking the spikes on his back into the floor, leaving tread marks, continuously vomiting from the speed by which he arrives anywhere.

SONIC THE COKE MULE

(Experiencing withdrawal) Woohoo, someone's been burning their barf at both ends. Y'all are like: oh no, my rations are looking at

me! I'm dizzy ever since I laid bacon in utero. I tied C-4 to the litter where I withdrew. The roadkill of my forebearers wore no collar. Dash through mom and find bonus pellets. They slammed her quill in a car door. *(Trips from trying to walk slow, recovers)* Not to challenge the stars, because I am their footnote, but the vanity of astrology is it tutors your genitals to behave in 2D. Am I at the behest of a substantial couple of empaths? You go joint by the pixie stick and no one will select you. We could handshake, but I'm etymologically frightened by the term broheim and there's a playground on the tip of your tongue. Pronouns originate from me calling you a buttmunch. I have to globetrot to catch my retch before it time travels. I crave the blur. You won't hold me captive, surgeon of forests, accelerating my chum across the screen of your hyperbolic chamber. I only fan out my pedigree if you buy me some fast food. I was marketed to never reciprocate. But say we're snorkeling this evening, then I can wince. *(Michael Jackson, The Prince of Crack scrapes powder off his arm, luring Sonic the Coke Mule to snort it off of him while dodging being petted)* Drumroll, please! Every logo should inspire racism. *(Pointing at Cop)* Is he the dildo you write home about? Strap him apt. Do some pro-life ninjutsu with me. Your feeling so safe sounds like bad porn. You rode a bus once? Alas! Getting to know you sucks. *(Sniffs Cop's crotch, heartily)* Is this the rubric where babies happen? These somnambulistic vinegars are the ones in charge? It's like how dogs think they shit their own legs so they can walk faster. I gargled the wrong priceless marathon. You can't count my swish. The emeralds I've inserted into my body endorse existentialism. I preside over a separate economy because I stay so anally palpable I can't sit down. Shit, I used to jog up waterfalls, spill my engagements, and die twenty times per board. The proceeds went to spreading HIV. Follow me! I will ride his camel toe into muteness. I want to point out which of his genes didn't pass muster.

Sonic the Coke Mule spins on the floor, revving himself, and darts out of the warehouse, leaving a trail of smoke and spike indentations. Michael Jackson, the Prince of Crack despondently stares after him, superimposed cross dissolve two shot of him in close up with himself, melodramatic pose.

MICHAEL JACKSON, THE PRINCE OF CRACK

He clamps to suggestive outerwear. If my heart could pause. The fiend. He's so sylphlike my hydraulics are obtuse. He set a grade of boundaries based on suicide. I'll mooch off him yet. He binges on gravity till it transforms focus groups nomadically aloof. His pleas will brighten my parlor. Then the basking shall convene. Does he know I ogle him with quarantine quality insights? I vote myself his slippery paraphernalia. I wanna bookmark his bacteria. My gundog has contracted such a righteous wool. Never fall for your coke mule. Aren't I the parcel he bumps? Dismantle me until we're both employees of the same sodomized heap. Shh, your vertebrae become doves in preschool. A bevy euthanize themselves to rhyme beside your amnesia. *(Weeping)* To the person you love, you're a cameo at best. If anyone sees who you are and chooses to remain with you, kill them with their own stilts. When he leaves me unrequited, the fog machines break down. Me and him are like doing the dishes with a price gun. We're so bottomed out on candy our cavities went to court and blamed us for meals altogether. I feel sparse inside the tuxedo. You should get to know your tissue, Willy, or the face might run right off your face. Sonic thinks you being tubby entails a PhD. You better not let him hop on you. He's mine to burn rubber with. I covet the floors he mars. Scoot after my snickerdoodle's dainty trail…'straight on till morning'. Reunite us as a family, drab as expectations. I'll deliver him a popsicle to share and yours will foreclose on her nail polish. If that girl had a plug at the end of her abortion, the walls would dimple in sympathy. Take the hearse. Since you have the aura of a skateboard crash.

Sir William Forsythe pats Period Sex Fred on the shoulder, signals a few henchmen, leaving the rest behind, points at Sonic the Coke Mule's trail and takes a toothpick out of his mouth, poking through the dress, resting it in Cop's cheek.

EXT. FREEWAY OVERPASS

Sir William Forsythe in a large black hearse, backseat, window side, benchmen next to him and driving. They are stuck in traffic.

SIR WILLIAM FORSYTHE

We remove the heart of a sixth grader on our anniversary. I'll dismember her conquests till we're of a magnitude. A carbon copy endowment, lynching her into affection. She'll splash in the fruit of her savior, celebrate each slit tummy I scrunch to hers. Hell will unglue its kennels! Unable to resuscitate the stocks we stuffed him drippy with, a discotheque dawdling between the horns, Satan will ponder the offerings we coronate in his purse and slink back into heaven on hands and fucking knees!

HENCHMAN 1

Boss?

SIR WILLIAM FORSYTHE

WHAT!?

HENCHMAN 1

Transit issue.

SIR WILLIAM FORSYTHE

Sorry. Can't pee without budgeting my romance. Funny, all the draining we need. Tingles when I make. Bitch must have the snapper of a doe. Soiling yourself is the only valid emotion. Drive faster, my AIDS is gaining on me.

HENCHMAN 2

(Whispering to driver) Is this a storybook overdose or does he actually wallow?

HENCHMAN 1

(Nervous) No clue what the man says. That's why we worship him.

A cup of soda hits the window.

WOMAN

(Trying to merge) Let me in, asshole! You're not important!

SIR WILLIAM FORSYTHE

(Leans between them, they jump) You have to cope with how often my prostate chimes in. Because I stomp seed up those who cope. *(Eurythmics —Somebody Told Me plays on radio)* Turns out we have an opening.

Sir William Forsythe gets out of the car and stands staring into the woman's window. She rolls it up. He motions for her to roll it back down, presses his mouth against the glass.

SIR WILLIAM FORSYTHE

Better hope you land facedown for the news crew.

Sir William Forsythe shoots the window, flattens a space over the webbing, and grabs the struggling woman by her hair, causing an infant strapped in the backseat to cry. Sir William Forsythe runs the head of the shouting woman over the remaining glass and guillotines it between the car door and the hot barrel of his gun, shooting her so her brains dart down the outer section of the car, her throat portioned by shards.

SIR WILLIAM FORSYTHE

(Observes traffic) Anyone standing in line was taught how to speak by their circumcision.

Sir William Forsythe snatches the toddler booster seat out of her car, carrying it as he opens fire on drivers and people who run. The henchmen stare, blank-faced, before cheering and following suit, sticking their weapons into backseats and firing on children balled up to hide: some dash or mumble pleas, reasoning, hands up, some freeze in horror. One man returns fire and they quickly surround and incapacitate him. Sir William Forsythe closes the man's head in a car hood. A tide of blood stains its way down the slanted overpass. They are all covered. Sporadic cries as his henchman finish off a few wounded. Sir William Forsythe takes a gigantic cell phone from a henchman and holds it up.

SIR WILLIAM FORSYTHE

Call your loved ones! Summon your hot little orphans! I want them to hear you bleat!

Sir William Forsythe smacks a woman with the phone until she, trembling, dials a number with it mashed against her and the tongue is blasted out of her head as soon as someone answers. His henchman are huddled over a family they've dragged around, taking turns circumcising them. Sir William Forsythe chucks the wailing booster seat off the overpass, skeet shooting it before it slams atop a passing car.

SIR WILLIAM FORSYTHE

How many fathoms to my vasectomy before the duet's complete? Brace yourselves: *(leans back in exaggeration)* muahahaha!

HENCHMAN 2

(The rest laughing hysterically) I wasn't that borderline sick with tension since my sister snuck into my room during a thunderstorm. Stress relief 101, sir!

HENCHMAN 1

Don't spoil the moment, you answering machine of a man.

Barking nearby. Sir William Forsythe searches for and removes a carriage, splaying a puppy onto the hood of a car, cutting off its floppy ears with a razor, mutilating and gathering its severed limbs, refining them into a bloodied granulation along the blade, piercing chop sounds against hollow car metal, snorting a section of its meat like cocaine.

SIR WILLIAM FORSYTHE

I can only get high off obituaries and pit bull sugar.

ULTIMATE ROT

(Promo in wild boar sounds) Ahhh, Wil-liam For-sythe, drop the waffles and answer this philosophical inquiry, if your thoughts aren't scratch and sniff…

Ultimate Rot stands silhouetted by headlights, back turned to them, flexed and rippling, fist raising slow for emphasis, steroid needles dangling.

HENCHMAN

Oh, fuck me with my own whole head.

ULTIMATE ROT

Should I break my thumbs before obtainment dilutes me or beam under the cargo of my kilt, genuflecting to roses as if their nutrition were gospel? The gods scoffed when I forged your waiver. I hobbled and boarded each of them, having never met a cripple who wasn't ubiquitous. Down my spleen they slid, crying out to you, William For-sythe! Prepare to lick the crumbs of your palace. Ground zero is just the calligraphy enjoyed below each cockpit. I see your supplements have receded. Are you the blimp for sale inside sewers? You sprained your neck finding god and it was only a manhole cover. Teddy bear hugs his victims like sexual fried chicken, but soon you will share their precipitous equalities. Same corpse, different cosmetics. Do you pray to your saddle? Is it yours through the stink? You are astride yourself in opposing firmness. I bet you've picked a coliseum into your nostril. Your undercarriage will not suffice. I petition against battered lads multiplying their agony across womankind. Perfect tits, extravagant gash, terminal velocity ass, a 'put 'em on the glass' intimacy, so you gotta feed her casket coins. Rub your catchphrases together for a lifespan. Anyone who owns a toothbrush is banal, but some still make their gums bleed every night. You just bought a second pair of glasses for the space where your balls aren't. Villain, you procured the paunch, but forgot to put a house under it. Busting Hitler poses at the mall? Don't you know love fizzles unless it can survive a plan? Reality pans its own boob job. It bowwows in the interrogative. You're supposed to be the bitch that dies alone. I've signed the paperwork to ensure your visage stays abridged. When I bench the burgeoning cancan deities from the terrain of your sacrifice, each death throe will feel eminently tailored. There are no caveats to rigor mortis. Until we're guppies latched by the leaving. Stow the feces an alright mercy. Some species to the shit you took. If you could suck your own silence, it would deny the semen. Quit sealing the bible with cocaine. Your veins are on sabbatical in a bucket, cardiovascular abbreviation! They form an unknown fealty. The pang in your nethers is from discount poison. Somebody's swimming trunks torpedoed the fridge. Don't make me titter till I'm discontinued. You chug wantonly and frequent your petunia. But I was shipped here to water the flowers in your knife hole. You don't command the antibodies to oust me. I'm the dope bout of anemia you can cling to now. An elite dosage, the consistency of which pioneered you in a septic tank. Reckon with bulimia hopscotch through the farmland, because my madness has deltoids. The chosen one's dispose-all vagina squats on porcupines like an identity. You fumbled your reflection. Let's stand our jinxes next to one another's. I was the ape who accused tools of being fake. You're the sort of warrior who takes up baking when he wins. I'm about to cobble you one lung. The forecast calls for reincarnation beneath my boot. You will stumble into faith. I'll make you potty in your cast. We'll be the environmental scribble people weep for via satellite. Who put a pothole in your diaphragm, Wil-liam For-sythe? I could facilitate a charity while dislocating the stitches in your anus. I'm so phobic I wear out my Pop-Tarts. My bangs are too low for a colonoscopy to work. But climb in till I'm on your taste buds. We'll be the hive that impacts its stir-stick. I'm going to balance a tennis ball on your lap and step on it until it's inside you. I'll fuck you with a phone book until everyone can record your scream. I stepped on my cheerleaders. Alert the ER.

SIR WILLIAM FORSYTHE

Welcome to the human compost party. Would you like to argue? We supposed to high five about that our cum works? You belong on a census. Meter maid went anabolic and begot the source of traffic. He's drowning in his grin. Knock that smile down his throat.

Sir William Forsythe motions for two of the four henchmen to attack. They open fire. Ultimate Rot remains still. They brandish razors and run toward him, dwarfed by his size. Ultimate Rot turns at once and explodes their heads together, splintering their skulls, eyes flying from their sockets, tongues knotting midair, brain matter adorning him like a t-shirt, and charges Sir William Forsythe. The other two Henchmen hide.

SIR WILLIAM FORSYTHE

(*Shooting*) Whoa, whoa, whoa, whoa, whoa! Hey, man, nevermind!

ULTIMATE ROT

(*Snatches gun, observes it, breaks in his fist*) What Neolithic pandering. You are based on what?

Ultimate Rot flings Sir William Forsythe into a car door. The door snaps free and molds around Sir William Forsythe's backside like a tortoiseshell as he stands up, trying to breathe, and uses the metal to block the next barrage of punches, backing away, grabbing corpses from cars and holding them up for Ultimate Rot to snatch out of his hands and smash apart. Another police helicopter spotlights them. A sniper shoots Ultimate Rot between the shoulder blades. Ultimate Rot swats at the wound, his skin purples, his veins bulge so tight the blood is rejected from leaking out of him, and he peels the car door off Sir William Forsythe's back, launching it into the helicopter, which crashes, obscuring them in smoke. Ultimate Rot lifts Sir William Forsythe off his feet, eye-level, single-handedly. Before Ultimate Rot can speak, Sir William Forsythe sneezes puppy fur into his eyes, slicing the streamers tied around his biceps. Ultimate Rot's skin changes from purple to gray, his heart decaying in translucent throbs, blood previously held in place sprinkling off, and he curls into rigor mortis, posed like The Thinker. Sir William Forsythe beckons his henchmen from hiding, feinting to slap them, and removes chainmail from under his trench coat, spitting and gasping in pain. The three of them drag Ultimate Rot to the overpass ledge and shove him off, with difficulty.

SIR WILLIAM FORSYTHE

He placed his ear on seashells and all he could hear was a police radio. He might have exploded with professional versatility, but if a throw pillow of him floats up, in ascension, strumming a harp, shoot the fucking thing out of his pork.

INT. FORMER PURR WAREHOUSE

Cop staring at Henchman through the dress.

COP

Suppose I've donned my bathroom break?

Henchman walks over, pulls the dress off Cop's head and replaces it with a bucket.

COP

Cute. Implication being my spout has a narwhal awrah. It does scare boy scouts.

Cop leans forward. The bucket drops between his feet.

HENCHMAN

(Unzips Cop) Get in line, fellas.

COP

You invite a spotter to unbuckle your britches, son?

HENCHMAN

Is that a…flipper?

Cop smiles, revealing broken teeth. Yellow pellets drop out of his pants and land loud in the bucket. His teeth begin pushing themselves out of the gums, restored in bloody spurts as long, razor sharp shark teeth. Cop kicks the bucket at Henchman, chews off his ropes, and kills three surrounding henchmen, before standing.

HENCHMAN

Taking applications for an informant, sir?

COP

Sorry, that position is filled.

Cop bites Henchman's face, shredding forehead to chin, swallowing his nose. Henchmen across the warehouse seem reluctant. A Ferrari crashes through the delivery gate, killing them. Streamline Crockett and Tubs steps out, two heads, sharing sentences, dressed in expensive pastels and jewelry, sunglasses. Cop wraps faceless Henchman in a blanket. He is breathing red bubbles through his caved in face. Cop taps him.

COP

You okay, buddy? *(Whispers)* This is Morse code for navigating Hades.

STREAMLINE CROCKETT AND TUBS

How do you crap on a butterfly? Wait till it ain't looking?

COP

I have, on my knee, the quintessential partner.

STREAMLINE CROCKETT AND TUBS

Hey, pal, had you lowered yourself to any exposition, we wouldn't be here, all expenses paid. You boiled over by the job?

COP

My man's recycled all the workman's comp. *(Gives the face hole a peck)* I exhibit OCD unless you daub my gills with cocoa butter.

STREAMLINE CROCKETT AND TUBS

Brass is going to pin you in a gold straightjacket and I'll applaud the shambles, nevertheless.

COP

Any applause should be nevertheless. I'm just the suppository my ventriloquist dummy backfired. Maybe he asked god too many questions.

Cop inches the skin rooted up, tendon by tendon, from Henchman's screeching neck and throws the head behind him into a garbage can, without looking.

STREAMLINE CROCKETT AND TUBS

I thought tongue cohered to asshole with minor obstacles in between, but no paper airplane could be that pretentious, padre. When Escobar Jr.'s companion grows restless peppering herself a homo, because blood oaths are fairly common law, she'll be back, en masse. Gal crowds her closet.

COP

(Hugging decapitated Henchman) Nothing more dangerous than a woman don't know what she wants, or a man that does. They'll meet at this location to fuck to death with my son between them.

STREAMLINE CROCKETT AND TUBS

Coldblooded genius, trawling with your loved ones. Confirm for me that ozone depletion isn't a fucking win win scenario to you.

COP

Christ sake, kid's ten and white. He'll scale his bootstraps. Tired of him skulking around, hinting he likes baseball. Besides, that cartoon hindrance trying to diddle him punches like he lost a custody battle.

Period Sex Fred rips duct tape off his head, balls it up, and throws it at the rafters. They ignore him. Michael Jackson, the Prince of Crack, descends.

MICHAEL JACKSON, THE PRICE OF CRACK

What's the going rate on them piranha chompers? You queens weren't supposed to whittle his personnel statewide in your rudder. Please, the semblance of an undisturbed vicinity. I'm your turncoat, not your matron. Judas couldn't have been a tenth as tantalizing.

COP

Judas fountained in his toga for a minute, when I rang.

STREAMLINE CROCKETT AND TUBS

(Grabs Michael Jackson, The Prince of Crack by the pant leg and yanks him down) Fairy's adept at being uppity through the net. You know, most conversations make me wish I had had SIDS. Me and the missus used to gamble with a laced pacifier. She likes loogies on her cleavage. *(Removes a vial)* I recall you're partial to vice dust.

MICHAEL JACKSON, THE PRINCE OF CRACK

(Sighs) Your fashion designer's fleas are spending themselves. *(Distracted by vial)* Of course transcendence comes in a can. But my booboo Sonic and I will be stationed together in a protected cabin, right? Doesn't your plot start with slavery? Several layups later, I'm glad to abet. I'd be in suspense, if I weren't diagnosed autistic.

COP

(Approaches, holding Henchman, his head in place) You two want off the grid? Normally, the grid zooms back to claim you. Your vermin might hatch a fond shampoo.

MICHAEL JACKSON, THE PRINCE OF CRACK

(Squeaks in terror) Is this bad cop, genocide cop? You guys communicate by the salary, yes? My modus operandi is a special recipe for dodo. We just wanna bait the sunset.

STREAMLINE CROCKETT AND TUBS

I can grant you tons of exclusivity at the morgue. *(Sprinkles vice dust)*
Are you in a gallery yet?

Michael Jackson, the Prince of Crack foams over as the dust lands on him, his suit expanding at the shoulders, face changing into David Byrne, His Squire by Force.

DAVID BYRNE, HIS SQUIRE BY FORCE

(Lurching backwards) You are pouring gasoline into someone's menopause because the nursing home sent a boiler plate rejection letter. You mean to pound bananas with the jocks like a doo wop nuzzler proud of the architectural superiority of his concussion, but the staff took turns blowing their brains out against a tacky spot of wallpaper. Flying over volcanoes for a living aged you prematurely because the temptation to frisk yourself inside one was habitual as twilight. You redefined escape before the massacre became a topography. Your fiancé divides herself within congested entities. Instead of touching you, she homogenizes her metacarpals until fellatio. In relationships, you're like an ant jerking off under a magnifying glass. Go on a diet till your halo fits. Pratfall through that bugger and pin it to the canvas. Pockmarks on the aria, bitten in the trendiest of gulags. Executing a chore deprecates your higgledy-piggledy past.

More dust lands, intense seizure, morphing into Ian Curtis, His Squire

By Force.

IAN CURTIS, HIS SQUIRE BY FORCE

I chop down trees with my heartbeat. Razing metropolises to calculate the globe. Add another round of barbed wire under my robe. I only idolize you to chew your feet. Better chance if we depart the womb on fire. My corneas underwent liposuction to dissolve your image. I sifted through your mother's scrimmage and came back holding a tire.

COP

It appears he resisted his bidet. *(Grabs Michael Jackson, the Prince of Crack's face until it settles)* Peter Pussy, assure me your treacheries matter. Not to tease an albino, but I have a bias for pigment.

MICHAEL JACKSON, THE PRINCE OF CRACK

(Weeping, experiencing crack shivers) Please impale me on my doll. Please finalize caresses from dolly! Anything!

COP

Don't piss in my aquarium and tell the fish it's vitamins.

STREAMLINE CROCKETT AND TUBS

(Sunglasses down on both heads) Places everyone.

INT. LAURIE ANDERSON, THE ONE AND ONLY'S WAREHOUSE

Laurie Anderson, the One and Only and Purr nude, carried upon flowing sheets, tummies pressed, post-coital. Menstrual Cult coo and fan them with banners of fluttering silk all around like the parachute game. Purr places a coke mirror over her bellybutton.

LAURIE ANDERSON, THE ONE AND ONLY

(Kisses her ear) You came like you were in a hurry. I'm forced to cross examine my edibles, if they're this delish.

PURR

I like you, but I can't be everyone's private arcade or I fool myself into thinking golf is commendable.

LAURIE ANDERSON, THE ONE AND ONLY

Avail yourself of regimental scrutiny when we're not afraid together, mon petit commando.

PURR

I'm several stories dumb.

LAURIE ANDERSON, THE ONE AND ONLY

Haven't we soared beyond you parodying your own monologue? Am I the precursor to your masochism? You are dishonest when you balk at our exception.

PURR

He asserts that too.

LAURIE ANDERSON, THE ONE AND ONLY

I try to stop myself and own you next to the moment, but I'm destined to be a convict in it, haggling with my stripes. *(They laugh)* You should do a touchdown with the remote control, if you're going to laugh at me. I'll convert to husbandry, least the metaphor buoys our incest. *(Coughs up her voice modulator)* Imagine practicing kegels against your will forever. That's me when I can't bother your mascara. We were like shish kabob on the devil's tail and she formed her signature through us. Are your lids hooded in solicitous vision because you sense that you are impervious to your prey?

PURR

No nest measuring. I seldom jet spray.

LAURIE ANDERSON, THE ONE AND ONLY

(Licking Purr's legs, her ankle wound) Wear me like a rachitic rosary against the pasture.

PURR

Silly pressures.

Laurie Anderson, the One and Only snorts lines off the coke mirror on Purr's tummy, then springs up, punching the glass, fracturing it without cutting her, and picks each individual piece from Purr's bellybutton with her mouth. Purr gasps in pleasure. Menstrual Cult gasps. Purr's bellybutton fills with a singular droplet of blood. Laurie Anderson, the One and Only slurps it.

LAURIE ANDERSON, THE ONE AND ONLY

(Teeth red) Epochs stutter between my 'I love you' and your avoiding a reply.

PURR

A motto premediated since it hushed the dinosaurs.

LAURIE ANDERSON, THE ONE AND ONLY

(Holding last mirror shard like a cigar) Humor me with devotion. Rejuvenate the blunder. Voice your carcinogens.

PURR

No.

LAURIE ANDERSON, THE ONE AND ONLY

(Cracks the glass in her mouth, bleeding heavily, Menstrual Cult drops them and screams) Which philanthropy so DECEIVED you that you would CONDONE such an ADULATORY juggling of accomplices without fretting possible RETALIATION on our behalf?! Pardon, I exert an uncharacteristic bravado when you spurn me.

PURR

(Dressing as she leaves) You're pathologically snarling down my span of the slide.

LAURIE ANDERSON, THE ONE AND ONLY

(Weeping, lisping) We blubber upon endless fortunes, our patience lapsing for the familiar ingrate fed by expired reveries!

PURR

Yeah, I'm on a shopping spree at the crematorium. I elapse at the bodega and flinch like a customer. Are there sentiments unscathed by wages? My amends rarely involve me.

LAURIE ANDERSON, THE ONE AND ONLY

(Flinching as Purr exits, spitting blood) Buxom fugitive! I'll supply you your freedom with a fucking embalmment! You'll be my bitch fixture! My sultriest taxidermy! You won't have the benefit of putrefaction! You filed for insolvency because a peck on the cheek was unreasonable!? Your default maniac is going to tackle you soon as you start twitching!

CLASSIC MAX HEADROOM

(Flickering on, having peeped at them) Perhaps modify the remedy, shabby as those are.

Laurie Anderson, the One and Only twirls nude at Classic Max Headroom, slashing in his direction with her violin bow, lacerating his face inside the screen, and punches through the glass of the giant monitor, swallowing the pieces as they fall on her, spitting shards whenever she speaks, new voice modulator. Menstrual Cult, weeping, bump into one another in confusion.

CLASSIC MAX HEADROOM

(Fizzled, dying through speakers) Eulogize me with the right cutlery. I secretly admired you how only a studio could.

LAURIE ANDERSON, THE ONE AND ONLY

Set your features! Aspirate upon request! We're about to go jousting with our trocars!

Menstrual Cult remove their tampons in unison and paint their faces with the blood. Laurie Anderson, the One and Only wraps her body in gauze veils, glowing red, and rises into a hoovering float, yelling as she leaves, followed by Menstrual Cult.

EXT. STREET

Purr stalking back toward her warehouse. No chopper sound. A passing squad car stops next to Purr, then reverses down the street. Hundreds of men surround Purr, bums, street thugs, and recently fired Wall Street brokers in disheveled suits, holding duffel bags and two by fours.

RECESSION ZOMBIE

Someone's daddy fucked her in the story before bedtime.

Purr shoves a pinkie in the corner of Recession Zombie's eye and chisels a symbol on his face with the other. Recession Zombie backs into the crowd, grabbing, starting a domino effect until everyone moves when Purr waves her free hand.

PURR

Shoo-in for a botched lobotomy, chat up my baby wipes, stock-pile the inmost supper as a podium and straddle it through coach. *(Plucks out his eyeball and spits into the socket, causing the fluids to hiss and curdle into a new warped pupil)* Show me your gums, so I can bless them! Giddy up!

The men, stuck wearing shit-eating grins, follow her.

EXT. COP FAMILY WAREHOUSE

Sir William Forsythe, sunken-eyed, shivery, swatting bugs, and his henchmen stand before another warehouse, where Sonic the Coke Mule's tracks end. The tracks turn into pooling blood, small limbs, and burst condoms of excrement and cocaine rolled into rings. Sonic the Coke Mule was shot and came to an unprepared halt, dismembering himself.

SIR WILLIAM FORSYTHE

We'd have to be debriefed by a conspiracy theorist to figure how kablooey he went.

Without a sound and within a second, according to their height, Hench-

man 1's head explodes, Henchman 2 is shot in the shoulder and Sir William Forsythe is shot in his upper chest. Henchman 2 tugs him into an alley. Sir William Forsythe stumbles, unstrapping a Kevlar vest.

HNECHMAN 2

(Picks the bullet out of his arm) Government issued. *(Tastes it)* Spiked with *(face becomes a smear, voice deepens, staggers around)*…belladonna?

SIR WILLIAM FORSYTHE

My stepson's bodyguard thinks I'm the redhead. All that pipsqueak's imaginary friends are about to pull a train on him. His hymen has an aroma so fierce I wanna draw a chalk outline around it and jump in. He'll expel my fetus out his bung and we'll ensconce a necklace of the fossil ricocheted between us while another sibling encores! PURR! Have my depravities regaled you!? Because you contain their bliss in a fucking shoebox! Wonder if she passes away impressed. I have to believe in the future or my bowels will halt.

INT. COP FAMILY WAREHOUSE

CIA Bill Duke, standing on an elevated walkway, turns from the window, silenced pistol smoking in one hand, screeching nightingale in the other, and addresses Cop Son: ten years old, wearing a business suit and holding a boombox to his ear.

CIA BILL DUKE

When I was born, the doctor slit my throat to see if I could talk. Too chilly outside to knock boots without a halo. I stripped the bolt I was strewn from in honor of mattresses. My parents stoked me into gestation with a single teardrop. Welfare distributed the ghetto scant bodily fluids. You had to stash the rundown on your thigh before it froze. Parents are there to sully the silence. They indicated height difference throughout childhood by smearing my placenta on a door. The crucifix above them had one of those hair metal front men fastened to it, looking like a reptile guffawing at secretions and who appreciates the WD-40 in his wrists. I turned in moms and pops for not scooping up some ofay's tobacco curd with their marriage certificate. Wall Street went haywire on Depends the weekend my intussusception solidified. Hyena entrails will blast out of a cannon during my twenty-one gun. You should ignore me. You'll learn something. *(Nightingale shrieking)* Oh, my beeper's angry. *(Unclips a beeper and gently stoves in the nightingale's head, collapsing the beak inward until just the beeper is sticking out of its body)* Now it can fly. Burial would be redundant for most anyone. There's a malfunctioning drawbridge below the plumage you must disconnect in order to gain rank. Once we grunted, we were a stable, except the uniform we invented to distract ourselves from restrooms kept needing an upgrade. Divulging an inch of who we are to one another put a legal kibosh on the mystery of life. People have more style under lava. We're a mildew ferns drooled off and regretted.

Sir William Forsythe has rolled Cop Wife in a wheelchair up the stairs to the walkway and leans over her, as if at a lecture. Henchman 2 faces the corner.

SIR WILLIAM FORSYTHE

Proceed. I forfeit you my continence.

CIA BILL DUKE

I find an individual becomes quite amenable when potential witnesses dry up. No self-confidence deserves the remains beneath a person. I'm too suave for questions, but it would concern you pawning your remains. Human history invested in a slab of coke with borders. We thought our spew was hype. This towering crouch we deemed a stockade, like denouncing your own hide could plausibly exonerate you. Tiertenders for a facsimile, an automated phagocytosis scalding our telomeres into a burlesque of scruples, villages pimpled by the steeple. No one wants to fast forward through a war, our solitary hypothesis against the threat of immortality. We fall in love with the paddle before it whispers to our ass. Nations already cunctator: we should hit control alt delete as the fluorescents become visible, dip a toe in our mass grave, rumble outta daddy's nut before he honks at mom. Nations refine the stockade. The urge to recur petted in solidarity is a collective, outdated neurosis. Shit, my particles can't even find each other through a scope.

COP SON

Dude, we're a settlement on par with inflammation. Our westerly bloat's ashamed of the harness it will disbar you from for agreeing to reform. I flaunt the turtle power they dole me. It's like, what would my turgor deign do? Those missing an LLC from their leger are ordinarily corpulent. Liken appending a parachute to your blister with the possibility of a degree carrying renown. You, though, bid with me against the sun. I praise the sun for holding still. Did we fuck up snapping its picture or something? Digest us already, god. That's why I only tan in moonlight. I was into hostile takeovers before my knuckles could crack. *(Throws a wad of cash)* Can you shine my shoes medium rare? I foresee in the rag's assault acquisitions from you to uterus. Anything beneath me is magic. It would be most tubular if the room took a bath with me, if I'm desirably tight. I hold a funeral every time I flush. No one revolts because their storage is such an effective ballast. *(Slaps own ass)* Sanctuary's for the mentally incognito. Am I a fitting apprentice because I just build forts? I'm confused, are you guys bringing me a steak or am I the steak?

CIA BILL DUKE

Pagans pick an object as their flaw. *(Indicates gun barrel)* This is the microscope that reveals infinities. You can track us back to the soot palmed between matter and chronology and we'd still be sputtering into a duplicate shrug.

SIR WILLIAM FORSYTHE

(Puts break on Cop Wife's wheelchair and approaches) This motherfucker needs a detective to find his skid marks.

CIA BILL DUKE

(Punches Sir William Forsythe in the throat and throws him through the window) Fucker, my entropy's got lace. All the police dogs know him. Their hydrant has an afterglow. He's more appealing from a distance. Genghis Khan was insecure about his cup size. Certain shell shock emits fresh minerals.

COP SON

(Blaring rap on boombox) I put hydraulics on my gonad. Is this racket how you people eavesdrop on your descendants? I feel fated to spar with my bong.

CIA BILL DUKE

Better scour your paraphernalia with sticky lint or I'll nibble us thermally defunct. What I grovel for is classified. They're transferring my pension to a less benign solar system. Temper's too glandular for babysitting.

SIR WILLIAM FORSYTHE

(Stumbles upstairs, shaking off glass, plucking shards out of his face) Am I the astronaut of my own jissom? Hope a lot of relatives pine tonight. You just stepped between me and the shelter cooze I'm poaching. Gonna play your colostomy bag like a guitar.

CIA BILL DUKE

(Kicks Sir William Forsythe in the knee as he approaches and throws him through the same hole in the window) Somebody should outlaw the narcotics in his skull. I'm beat about this unanimous rigging I enforce and am enforced by. I won't have met my quota until oil is our only wreath. *(Holds gun to head)* Naturalism concedes no alternate stance. I had my block under kinesthetic patrol. I could shoot the shadow off a kid. They obscure their hands on purpose. Hysterical, for the depth of a clip. I memorized enormous languages, so my supervisors assigned me to canonize the earth in snuff. We'll fuck harder when we're endangered. That's why this man's attempt

at fabricating domesticity from vulture dung won't ease his consort into a witting prolapse.

SIR WILLIAM FORSYTHE

(*Bleeding liberally, additional glass stuck all over his face and trench coat, limping up the stairs*) Jury's out on my wingspan, governor. You greedy to surpass the Richter scale? (*Kicks Cop Wife's wheelchair down the stairs. She lands horribly*) I do miss my termagant with elemental dominion. (*Counters a strike, going into a boxer hug with CIA Bill Duke, picking glass off himself and slamming a fistful down on top of his opponent's head*) Aha!

CIA BILL DUKE

(*Pivots and launches Sir William Forsythe back out the window as he moves for a follow up strike*) You think I can't pivot?!

COP SON

(*In the background, having torn a wheel from Cop Wife's wheelchair, sneaking up behind CIA Bill Duke, who is plucking glass out of his scalp, slamming the wheel around his neck, encasing him in broken spokes*) Your pants aren't regulation MC Hammer enough! Don't be a mark ass trick. Your momma so loose them labes queef to and fro like a doggy door. Yea, my dick so big they cancelled Christmas. Peace in the Middle East! (*Wrenches CIA Bill Duke's head and spine from the rest of his body, twisting the wheel, and adorns himself with the viscera like a mink stole, placing a purple crown air freshener over the hole in the corpse)* I take my furs in the larval state.

HNCHMN 2

(Grabs a fixture on the wall) I'm grappling with his sow of a wife, boss! If my spell had dice, she'd be thrown through it!

COP SON

(Taps Henchman 2, leading him outside by the hand, stepping on Cop Wife) Don't bother stepping over the matriarch. She's been evacuated to the point of wreckage. Swipe yourself on her matting, chief, as she's contrived my corridor into an oncoming, quadriplegic salmonella. Can't brown bag that much fucking overdue euthanasia. Best part about capping a police is if others like him sob.

HNCMN 2222

I'm zapped superlative by disqualified serpents. Are we runts under scrums, reoccurring archetypes of some fanged nostalgia? Dressing up in apocalypse? *(Cop Son reaches up to pat the bullet hole in his shoulder)* Exploding into a million pieces might help me go to the bathroom for once.

EXT. COP FAMILY WAREHOUSE

Sir William Forsythe lies in the middle of the street, in a pile of glass, freebasing.

COP SON

Will you goddamn never Siamese flex this beige keister? Aren't you here to sponge my young rectum with your beak?

SIR WILLIAM FORSYTHE

(Stands, wobbly, and rips out a huge chunk of his hair, holding it up) I have to wash this tonight.

COP SON

Uh-oh. Girly has a headache. I must negotiate my way out of the friend zone before daddy bigwig declines me a caning.

SIR WILLIAM FORSYTHE

(Snatches Cop Son's boombox) Lesson one: disappear into the eyes of your seducer and they will blink you out like the thousandth crab. You wanna test your lice as her fucking valet troop?

Sir William Forsythe tries to throw the boombox to skeet shoot it, but is too wounded. The boombox slides a few feet. Sir William Forsythe waits a beat, then shoots concrete several times until a bullet reaches the boombox.

CAMCORDER POV

MISTER GONZO PORN

(VO) That a baby. Your bush gotta rowdy dew? Need a stampede to squirt? Should I back over your cunt with a limousine? Disintegrate the interior. Suck muffler while I gun the engine and drag you barren with some ecstatic frottage. I like shut-in pussy woozy from the flu. Girl, you look like you deserve to pass a stone. I'm facially blunt with those of an inferior stock. Bet you founder during cavity searches because that ass was elongated by a cinder block. Couple shipwrecks in your bottle. Bet if you hunkered down a fortnight you could get the bottom of a dumpster tasting like vanilla. Let's give our baby HPV when he winks. Hatchet snatch always reincarnates into itself again. Those tits could interrupt a picnic. Ooo, I'm thrumming in your shunt, stoma queen, two cigarettes below the waist. You my moist scum snagging garbage pail swing sets in them panties? Could you twirl a wrench with your cunt, grousing about blood loss as I brag? Should I dig up the Labradoodle from my childhood and fuck you with its wag? Flick that deceased vulva too cheap to rent, posthaste. Our lady of the shitstick only drinks from pools when your daughter's done. You have the posture of a snail in a headlock

70

because you're auditing your blockage. As strays go, you made the best seller list with a capital slut.

Sir William Forsythe interrupts Mister Gonzo Porn, popping his hand into a nearby residential mailbox with a symbol spray painted on it, and removes a bazooka. Silence, smash to black.

INT. (FORMER) PURR WAREHOUSE

STREAMLINE CROCKETT AND TUBS

(Holding police radio, parked by the rear entrance) Trudy, we whip this yayo freight into a bar of silicone and it'll erase all the typos inside you.

Sir William Forsythe, sooty, clothes singed, smoking bazooka strapped to his back, appears behind Streamline Crockett and Tubs, slitting both throats with a razor. Cop Son pretends to record everything, holding a destroyed camcorder with a severed penis stuffed through the lens. Henchman 2 in a daze.

SIR WILLIAM FORSYTHE

Double my fucking pleasure, yuppie. Who moans first moans last. Scuffed your duds. Dragnet's gargling its threads. Blood increases resale. Your conga line's salivating in limbo. *(Streamline Crockett and Tubs gurgling blood)* You sound hired.

MICHAEL JACKSON, THE PRINCE OF CRACK

(Descending, secretly gesturing toward Cop) How downright winsome a delight to have you revitalize our scene with vestal unity on this day of testosterone in summation.

SIR WILLIAM FORSYTHE

(Sighs) When can we exit the snitch age and enter the fatalities age? You and I suffer tandem lamentations. Sonic had a game over.

MICHAEL JACKSON, THE PRINCE OF CRACK

(Drops the rest of the way, long pause) Nuh-uh, Sonic had lives.

SIR WILLIAM FORSYTHE

(Hand on Michael Jackson, The Prince of Crack's shoulder) Out of guys, I fear. His oppressors were dealt with.

MICHAEL JACKSON, THE PRINCE OF CRACK

(Cold) The body?

SIR WILLIAM FORSYTHE

An inoperable squash. You could see for yourself, but the paramedic carted him off in her flask.

COP SON

(To Cop, aiming camcorder) Okay, you're not disappointed in me: action. I've venerated your estate with an eerie batch of Armani. You're the apex ornament at the summit of our family tree and my self-immolation will reimburse you. Now you're the glaring scrap lumber guided by strikes that have derecognized you in a huffy lockout my firm consulted and I'll be the smidge of come you should have wiped up with a coupon. Action.

COP

(Stands from chair, feigned bindings drop, voice octaves deeper) I revoke your flank for its yearning to be canoodled with by strangers. Peer down the iris as it garrotes you, boy. *(Snatches and bites through Cop Son's neck, removing the head, holding it high, Cop biting his own lips and chin completely severed until Cop's head collapses into his shoulders and his headless body sets Cop Son's head down in place, over gore strewn neck. Cop Son's head speaking in Cop's voice, growing shark teeth again)* You were improperly weaned.

Michael Jackson, The Prince of Crack screams. The television box snaps in half and falls off of him. Warehouse windows explode. In fast montage, Michael Jackson, The Prince of Crack throws on a red leather jacket equipped with giant studs and spikes, glow steps into lava-hot sparkling shoes, and whip-points at Cop, grabbing his own crotch until blood leaks

*out of his pants. Police, having surrounded the building, panic and open
fire.*

MICHAEL JACKSON, THE PRINCE OF CRACK

(Moonwalking through volley of bullets) YOU'RE NEXT ON MY
MOTHERFUCKING LOVE!

*Michael Jackson, The Prince of Crack cleaves through surrounding po-
lice, grating their faces to mush against his jacket, burning shoeprints
in their skulls with lightning fast kicks, dodging and deflecting bullets,
noises of robotic steam release.*

LAURIE ANDERSON, THE ONE AND ONLY

PURR!

*Laurie Anderson, The One and Only and Menstrual Cult stand revealed
behind fallen police. Purr and Recession Zombies face them from an entrance across the warehouse. Purr motions and both teams charge one
another, sticking remaining police with trocars, which shoot blood out
one end once flesh is penetrated, and smashing them with nail-wrought
boards as all open fire. Laurie Anderson, The One and Only, stalks unaffected through the mayhem, aiming her violin bow at Sir William
Forsythe, who has stood himself between her and Purr. Michael Jackson, The Prince of Crack moonwalks around Laurie Anderson, The One
and Only until she clotheslines him.*

MICHAEL JACKSON, THE PRINCE OF CRACK

(Recovers, dipping her in a ballroom dance grab) Sellouts redub their nerve endings. Right, diva?

LAURIE ANDERSON, THE ONE AND ONLY

(Spits glass in his face) My legacy will detonate legacies.

MICHAEL JACKSON, THE PRINCE OF CRACK

(Kisses her) TEE! HEE! That tickles!

Laurie Anderson, The One and Only leaps back, retching in disgust, and slices the jacket and skin off Michael Jackson, The Prince of Crack, exposing muscles stuffed with wet circuitry. Michael Jackson, The Prince of Crack moonwalks out of his entire skein, twirling blood in Claymation. Laurie Anderson, The One and Only, bends Michael Jackson, The Prince of Crack over her knee and slides the violin bow across his bones and sinew, playing him instrumentally, a strange and unsellable song. Everyone around them is murdered or murdering. Period Sex Fred, seeing Menstrual Cult, works himself into a petrified circling of honk sounds, screen flickering (the edges read 35mm), *tape flaking off, scalp flapping. Purr, locking eyes with Sir William Forsythe, holds Period Sex Fred, calmed by her touch, and inserts a pinkie into the base of his skull, easing him to the floor, a single tear in her eye.*

SIR WILLIAM FORSYTHE

His auntie decided to molest him on the densest flow of her cycle and Period Sex Fred thought their secret injured her, that he was at fault, a prepubescent sex murder. That's why I indulged him into existence as your playmate, because tragedy bonds us instantaneously. Though your inconsolable lonesomeness satirized my being there for you, IN PERPETUUM, you HAD to fuck our invisible cohort! I cooked you up a sidekick and you raped it because ennui. It's not that you fucked a bunch, it's that you never asked.

Period Sex Fred's body ages into a child's inside his clothes and evaporates.

PURR

(Quiet, but heard through the carnage) Realest aspect to him was how someone could finally dominate me. Your ace groom blew bubbles in my twat.

SIR WILLIAM FORSYTHE

I wish I treated you like a whore, instead of just calling you one after you broke me. I'm the type of sociopath they have to bury with his toys. Shit shan't vex, right? You went steady with your exercise bike, siphoning affirmative action spunk from a catalogue that could never eclipse us!

PURR

How were you possibly jealous? You're all the same fucking man to me. I can't cheat on you with yourself.

SIR WILLIAM FORSYTHE

No one can choose me over retardation. The two are exclusive! *(They laugh)* Being this sinister requires an exhaust valve. *(Takes a knee, shakily removes shattered crackpipe. It slips from his hand)* You would need references to go through withdrawal. Frame me around your toilet. My pledges establish match point runniness. Understand I cannot wain. I'm the caviar emptied out your acne. I've been squeezed handsomely ajar. Treat me like a cousin you can't neglect. You still my little sky high enema? That clit sure had sky. Gnarly width distinct amid slobber. None partake them dimples to evict me. We unwound each other's rat wounds across Paree. The comeback rooster started out decapitated. Honey, I inscribe your every locket with 'my bad!' I'm spilling in my pants faster than there's time. *(Extends hand to Purr)* Pretty fucking please?

PURR

This motherfucker mistook his tit milk for caviar. Burp on my clam. If you had anything but a hunk of gauze between your knees, I would write a fucking essay between the tape. That cock's so sweet

I cry wolf when I love you. Not every castration is this much of a procedure. You put science under a spatula and called it an orgasm.

SIR WILLIAM FORSYTHE

(Dabs his eyes and shoots a Recession Zombie hitting him over the back repeatedly with a board) You-you better completely censor me from your fucking psyche. Etch me out!

PURR

I pranked you into loving me, my lamest hustle. All you do is diminish my potency. Men reduced the alphabet to themselves. You improvised a vocabulary to constrain trim. I veto the debauchery charter. It is not my duty to disperse the want of others. My rapists have inherited the same mask, the same condom *(utters an insane hiss and punches herself, nose gushing)*, not that I deserve protection! Since you checkmated my crib, this cunt was an Indian giver, especially when you disgustingly mounted it! Guess Chicken Little won't survive his enema!

Purr lies down and scratches a large symbol into the floor with her pinkie, speaking backwards, until Horned Vanilla Ice rises.

HORNED VANILLA ICE

(To Purr) I scuttle down that booty to my master, having been

warned in the affirmative who it is I'm after.

RECESSION ZOMBIE #1

(Wall collapses) It's Grace Jones! Hit the deck!

RECESSION ZOMBIE #2

Whose side is she on?!

RECESSION ZOMBIE #1

Grace Jones's side!

A blur smashes through the warehouse, killing anyone who doesn't dive out of the way, trampling Horned Vanilla Ice (aroused as blur approaches) into a twitching pile, smashing through the wall opposite. Purr sighs. Laurie Anderson, The One and Only, distracted from her song, is poked through both eyes by Michael Jackson, The Prince of Crack's skeleton fingers, and they bleed out in a lump. Blood from the amount of ongoing combat flies into the rafters, splashing and blinding doves, causing them to fall. Lead Recession Zombie breaks a board in half over Henchman 2, the nail end hanging in his shoulder.

HCHCNNNNNNNNHCHCH2222222222222222222222222

(Grabs Recession Zombie) Whoa, commence mastication for the middleman of napkins. Loot can defecate its own motility, Pac-Man's

79

theory of natural selection. Our lucre pasted us together to referee a mutual filth. We even manufacture it an odor.

Henchman 2 sticks a penny in Recession Zombie's blood eye. Recession Zombies all begin vomiting pennies.

HHHHHHHHHHHHHHHHHHHHHHHHHHHHHHHHHHH-
HHHHHHHHH22222222222222222

(To Sir William Forsythe) Boss, she's either too big with her freedom or you backed the wrong pony, but how about that raise?

SIR WILLIAM FORSYTHE

Sure.

Sir William Forsythe points his finger at his own head like a gun and pulls the thumb trigger. Henchman 2's brains explode. Purr charges Sir William Forsythe, killing Recession Zombies.

SIR WILLIAM FORSYTHE

Ooo, I'm shakin' in my urinal! I haven't wept since the doctor slapped me, bitch. I lost you? Who didn't!? Don't think I'd spend less than a year cannibalizing the Ivy-League space behind those polyps. I'm simply the most persistent chump in the lineup between your sheets. Reliant on how much others decide I should love them? I decide a lot! I've been top shelf deprived. You have no clue if you want to fuck someone, unless you fuck them for a trimester.

Purr strikes out with her pinkies. Sir William Forsythe catches Purr's arms and lifts her into the air, admiring her.

SIR WILLIAM FORSYTHE

(Sets Purr down, gently) If I shit you an ode, it's for the sake of the ode.

Menstrual Cult tackles Sir William Forsythe, covering every visible inch of his body. Sir William Forsythe trudges through them, toward Purr.

SIR WILLIAM FORSYTHE

Pssst! Pssst!

COP

Here, sissy.

Cop slaps Purr to the floor. Sir William Forsythe bursts Menstrual Cult off of him, sailing them in every direction, blood squirting trocars dangling from his back. Cop snatches a Menstrual Cult midair, yanking her dress over her head, and audibly snaps her spine with both fists. Sir William Forsythe runs up Menstrual Cult's bent over corpse like a ramp, grabbing another Menstrual Cult by the ankle and slams her crotch-first down onto Cop's small head, knotting her legs around it. Huffing on the floor, Cop suffocates inside shrieking and dying Menstrual Cult, trying to eat his way out. Wading through blood, groaning wounded everywhere, Sir William Forsythe picks Purr up by her Mohawk. Purr spins on him and climbs, stabbing her pinkies into his clavicles, latching them. Sir William Forsythe lands on his ass, paralyzed, clutching Purr, her legs straddling his waist. Purr lets Sir William Forsythe kiss her until the kiss echoes. Sir William Forsythe turns, noticing Purr has broken off her pinkie fingernails in him, unstrapping and placing the muzzle of the bazooka directly against both of their heads.

SIR WILLIAM FORSYTHE

(Echoing) If you can't whistle through your wounds, they're not deep enough.

PURR

(Echoing) I succumbed to my wounds long ago.

SIR WILLIAM FORSYTHE

We used to press our STDs with a rock to memorialize each other. Only way you can trademark your fucking birth.

PURR

I demand chocolate chips inside my urn.

SIR WILLIAM FORSYTHE

Defile some angels for me, dear. Better fortify themselves with disinfectant.

PURR

May flies land on what we had together.

Sir William Forsythe is hugging Purr so hard her body cracks. Purr props her bare foot on the trigger guard, pulling the trigger with her toe. Blast in red flashes: their 16-bit splatter an engraved pixelation scrolling panel after panel down the wall behind them.

GAME OVER

Sean Kilpatrick wrote *Anatomy Courses* (with Blake Butler, Lazy Fascist Press), does monthly movie reviews for *Hobart*, and other works have appeared or are forthcoming in *Boston Review, Nerve, The Quietus, Fence, Vice, Sleepingfish, Bomb, Evergreen Review, Columbia Poetry Review, New York Tyrant, Obsidian: Literature & Arts in the African Diaspora, Black Sun Lit, The Malahat Review, Caketrain, Tarpaulin Sky, Exquisite Corpse, fluland, No Colony, La Petite Zine, Juked, The Volta, LIT, Jacket2, Whiskey Island, The Collagist, Action Yes, New South, KMSU Weekly Reader, The Talking Book, Fanzine, Dostoyevsky Wannabe, 30 Under 30, Dzanc Best of the Web 2010, HTMLGIANT,* and as a *Best American Essays 2014* notable.

www.ingramcontent.com/pod-product-compliance
Lightning Source LLC
Chambersburg PA
CBHW051309250626
47155CB00009B/3491